Rameses' Journey Through The Tar Heel State

Aimee Aryal

Illustrated by Blair Cooper

MASCOT BOOKS

www.mascotbooks.com

Rameses was enjoying his spring in Chapel Hill. He decided it would be a perfect time for a road trip around the great State of North Carolina. Rameses was looking forward to seeing many interesting sights all over the Tar Heel State, and making new friends along the way.

Before hitting the road, Rameses passed the Old Well, where several students saw him and waved. "Have a great trip, Rameses!" they called. Rameses also stopped at the Bell Tower. The mascot packed his bags, hopped into the Tar Heel Mobile, and was off!

From campus, the mascot headed to the North Carolina State Capitol in Raleigh. Rameses was impressed by the majestic building. At Capitol Square, Rameses saw UNC fans. "Rah, Rah, Carolina!" they shouted.

Chapel Hill, along with Durham and Raleigh, are the three cities that make up The Research Triangle, which is known for its great universities and high-tech companies.

Rameses then headed to the North Carolina Zoo. The mascot was happy to see so many interesting animals and learn about their habitats. At the lion's den, a big cat roared, "Hello, Rameses!"

The Greensboro Coliseum is often home to the ACC Basketball Tournament, which has been held annually since 1954.

Luckily for Rameses and all Tar Heels fans, the mascot arrived in Greensboro just in time for the ACC Basketball Tournament. Outside the Greensboro Coliseum, he posed for a picture with a young Tar Heels fan. Rameses was happy to see so many fans dressed in Carolina blue!

Rameses roamed the sidelines and inspired the basketball team with his spirit. Together with the cheerleaders, he led Tar Heels fans as they chanted, "Here Comes Carolina!" The Heels played great ball and beat their rivals from Durham.

With a few days off before the start of the
NCAA Basketball Tournament, Rameses
was back on the road, excited to see more
of the Tar Heel State.

Like most North Carolinians, Rameses loved
Bar-B-Q. He especially loved finding good
roadside Bar-B-Q! He ate a sandwich with
a new friend who was thrilled to spend time
with the mascot. "This is delicious,
Rameses," she said.

The town of High Point is America's furniture capital, with over 70 furniture stores.

Full from his big sandwich, Rameses drove to High Point, where he got a chance to see the world's largest dresser. It was huge! The UNC fans standing next to the dresser looked so small! "I don't have enough clothes to fill that," Rameses thought to himself.

Having just enjoyed some of the state's famous food, Rameses was still hungry — to learn about the state's history! He drove the Tar Heel Mobile to Old Salem, where he experienced life in colonial North Carolina. Dressed in his best colonial attire, Rameses strolled through Old Salem.

Even though Rameses was dressed in his UNC uniform, Carolina fans still recognized him! He saw a bunch of Tar Heels fans at Old Salem. A father and son waved and said, "Hello, Rameses!"

One of the oldest towns in the State of North Carolina, Old Salem, was founded in 1766.

Rameses' next stop was Asheville, where he toured the beautiful Biltmore Estate. He was amazed how huge the house was! During the tour, Rameses learned a lot about the house's construction and history.

At over 175,000 square feet, the Biltmore Estate in Asheville, North Carolina is the largest privately owned home in the United States of America.

After finding his way back outside, he joined a bunch of young Tar Heels fans for a friendly game of soccer. After the mascot scored, one of his teammates shouted, "Goal, Rameses!"

Rameses was eager to experience the great outdoors, so he drove through Great Smoky Mountain National Park. Rameses stopped at a famous mountain course for a round of golf, where he scored a hole-in-one! "Nice shot, Rameses!" said his playing partner.

Next, Rameses went fishing. He caught a big one! The worried fish said, "Hello, Rameses!"

Rameses thought it would be great to end the day with a hike through the mountain range. He watched the sunset from atop one of the park's many peaks. "It sure is beautiful here in North Carolina," he thought.

Charlotte is the largest city in North Carolina and is nicknamed "The Queen City."

From the wilderness, Rameses drove to Charlotte, the state's largest city. He loved looking at the city's gorgeous skyline, with all the tall buildings.

After cruising through downtown, Rameses headed to the Charlotte Motor Speedway and ended up on the track during a race! He drove the Tar Heel Mobile as fast as he could and even took the checkered flag! The mascot won the race and race fans chanted, "Go, Rameses, go!"

The Cape Hatteras Lighthouse is the tallest brick structure ever moved. After the ocean grew too close, it was moved a half-mile inland in 1999.

Rameses continued east all the way to the Atlantic Ocean. At Cape Hatteras, he stopped at the famous lighthouse, where he ran into more Carolina fans. "Hello, Rameses!" said the boys.

That night, Rameses joined a family for an old-fashioned cookout on the beach. The group roasted s'mores and swapped stories. The family was impressed to learn all about Rameses' journey around the Tar Heel State.

Rameses stayed on the Outer Banks for a trip to Kitty Hawk, the site of the Wright Brothers' historic "first flight." Feeling the spirit of the town's famous residents, Rameses went hang gliding over the Atlantic Ocean!

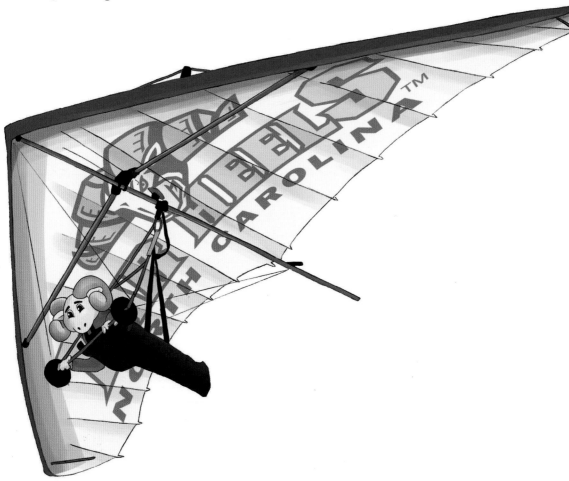

As he walked to the Wright Brothers National Memorial, he was surprised to see so many Tar Heels fans. "Hello, Rameses! Go, Tar Heels!" said a couple of the fans as they welcomed him to Kill Devil Hills. Soon, he was flying a replica of the same plane the Wright Brothers used! "That sure was scary!" Rameses thought after he landed.

Orville and Wilbur Wright were the first men to get a working airplane to fly. They accomplished the feat on December 17, 1903.

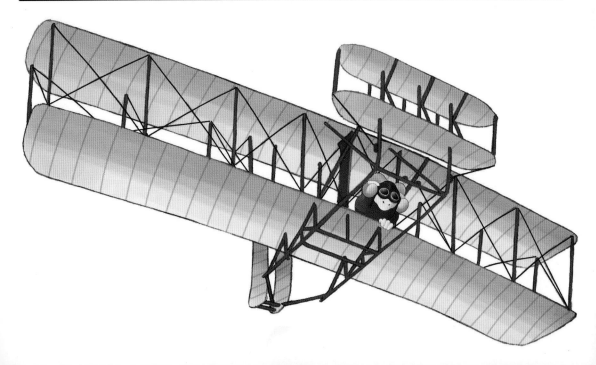

Rameses felt like relaxing in the sun, so he went to the beach. He made sure to put on a lot of sunscreen to protect his white fur from a sunburn! After taking a nap in his beach chair, Rameses decided to explore the sandy beach and was excited to see wild horses walking along the ocean. "Hello, Rameses!" they neighed.

Rameses knew he would have to head back to campus soon, so he jumped back into the Tar Heel Mobile to drive home, but he got stuck in the deep sand!

Finally, Rameses returned to Chapel Hill.
He thought about his great vacation and how
much he enjoyed seeing the Tar Heel State.
He was excited to return home and tell his
friends all about his journey and share his
beautiful pictures.

So long, Rameses!

Rameses'
Journey Through
The Tar Heel State

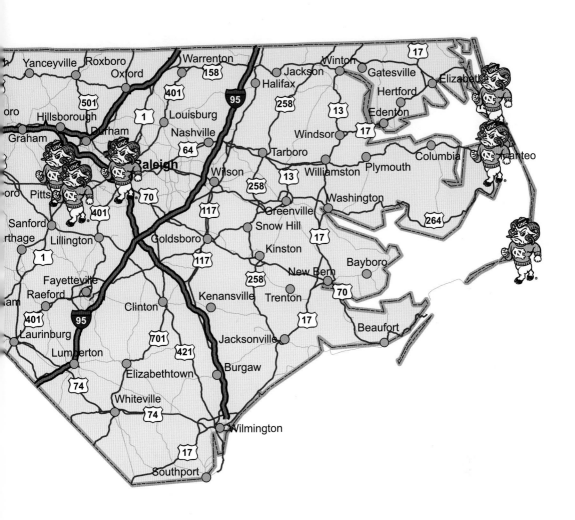

For Anna and Maya. ~ Aimee Aryal

For Jason Ray. ~ Blair Cooper

For more information about our products,
please visit us online at www.mascotbooks.com.

For more information, please contact Mascot Books,
P.O. Box 220157, Chantilly, VA 20153-0157

ISBN: 1-934878-20-0

Printed in the United States.

www.mascotbooks.com

MASCOT BOOKS

www.mascotbooks.com

Title List

Major League Baseball

Boston Red Sox	Hello, *Wally*!	Jerry Remy
Boston Red Sox	*Wally The Green Monster And His Journey Through Red Sox Nation*!	Jerry Remy
Boston Red Sox	Coast to Coast with *Wally The Green Monster*	Jerry Remy
Boston Red Sox	A Season with *Wally The Green Monster*	Jerry Remy
Colorado Rockies	Hello, *Dinger*!	Aimee Aryal
Detroit Tigers	Hello, *Paws*!	Aimee Aryal
New York Yankees	Let's Go, *Yankees*!	Yogi Berra
New York Yankees	*Yankees Town*	Aimee Aryal
New York Mets	Hello, *Mr. Met*!	Rusty Staub
New York Mets	*Mr. Met* and his Journey Through the Big Apple	Aimee Aryal
St. Louis Cardinals	Hello, *Fredbird*!	Ozzie Smith
Philadelphia Phillies	Hello, *Phillie Phanatic*!	Aimee Aryal
Chicago Cubs	Let's Go, *Cubs*!	Aimee Aryal
Chicago White Sox	Let's Go, *White Sox*!	Aimee Aryal
Cleveland Indians	Hello, *Slider*!	Bob Feller
Seattle Mariners	Hello, *Mariner Moose*!	Aimee Aryal
Washington Nationals	Hello, *Screech*!	Aimee Aryal
Milwaukee Brewers	Hello, *Bernie Brewer*!	Aimee Aryal

College

Alabama	Hello, Big Al!	Aimee Aryal
Alabama	Roll Tide!	Ken Stabler
Alabama	Big Al's Journey Through the Yellowhammer State	Aimee Aryal
Arizona	Hello, Wilbur!	Lute Olson
Arkansas	Hello, Big Red!	Aimee Aryal
Arkansas	Big Red's Journey Through the Razorback State	Aimee Aryal
Auburn	Hello, Aubie!	Aimee Aryal
Auburn	War Eagle!	Pat Dye
Auburn	Aubie's Journey Through the Yellowhammer State	Aimee Aryal
Boston College	Hello, Baldwin!	Aimee Aryal
Brigham Young	Hello, Cosmo!	LaVell Edwards
Cal - Berkeley	Hello, Oski!	Aimee Aryal
Clemson	Hello, Tiger!	Aimee Aryal
Clemson	Tiger's Journey Through the Palmetto State	Aimee Aryal
Colorado	Hello, Ralphie!	Aimee Aryal
Connecticut	Hello, Jonathan!	Aimee Aryal
Duke	Hello, Blue Devil!	Aimee Aryal
Florida	Hello, Albert!	Aimee Aryal
Florida State	Let's Go, 'Noles!	Aimee Aryal
Georgia	Hello, Hairy Dawg!	Aimee Aryal
Georgia	How 'Bout Them Dawgs!	Aimee Aryal
Georgia	Hairy Dawg's Journey Through the Peach State	Vince Dooley / Vince Dooley
Georgia Tech	Hello, Buzz!	
Gonzaga	Spike, The Gonzaga Bulldog	Aimee Aryal / Mike Pringle
Illinois	Let's Go, Illini!	
Indiana	Let's Go, Hoosiers!	Aimee Aryal
Iowa	Hello, Herky!	Aimee Aryal
Iowa State	Hello, Cy!	Aimee Aryal
James Madison	Hello, Duke Dog!	Amy DeLashmutt
Kansas	Hello, Big Jay!	Aimee Aryal
Kansas State	Hello, Willie!	Aimee Aryal
Kentucky	Hello, Wildcat!	Dan Walter
LSU	Hello, Mike!	Aimee Aryal
LSU	Mike's Journey Through the Bayou State	Aimee Aryal
Maryland	Hello, Testudo!	
Michigan	Let's Go, Blue!	Aimee Aryal
Michigan State	Hello, Sparty!	Aimee Aryal
Minnesota	Hello, Goldy!	Aimee Aryal
Mississippi	Hello, Colonel Rebel!	Aimee Aryal
Mississippi State	Hello, Bully!	Aimee Aryal

Pro Football

Carolina Panthers	Let's Go, Panthers!	Aimee Aryal
Chicago Bears	Let's Go, Bears!	Aimee Aryal
Dallas Cowboys	How 'Bout Them Cowboys!	Aimee Aryal
Green Bay Packers	Go, Pack, Go!	Aimee Aryal
Kansas City Chiefs	Let's Go, Chiefs!	Aimee Aryal
Minnesota Vikings	Let's Go, Vikings!	Aimee Aryal
New York Giants	Let's Go, Giants!	Aimee Aryal
New York Jets	J-E-T-S! Jets, Jets, Jets!	Aimee Aryal
New England Patriots	Let's Go, Patriots!	Aimee Aryal
Pittsburgh Steelers	Here We Go Steelers!	Aimee Aryal
Seattle Seahawks	Let's Go, Seahawks!	Aimee Aryal
Washington Redskins	Hail To The Redskins!	Aimee Aryal

Basketball

Dallas Mavericks	Let's Go, Mavs!	Mark Cuban
Boston Celtics	Let's Go, Celtics!	Aimee Aryal

Other

Kentucky Derby	White Diamond Runs For The Roses	Aimee Aryal
Marine Corps Marathon	Run, Miles, Run!	Aimee Aryal

Missouri	Hello, Truman!	Aimee Aryal
Nebraska	Hello, Herbie Husker!	Todd Donoho
North Carolina	Hello, Rameses!	Aimee Aryal
North Carolina	Rameses' Journey Through the Tar Heel State	Aimee Aryal
North Carolina St.	Hello, Mr. Wuf!	
North Carolina St.	Mr. Wuf's Journey Through North Carolina	Aimee Aryal / Aimee Aryal
Notre Dame	Let's Go, Irish!	
Ohio State	Hello, Brutus!	Aimee Aryal
Ohio State	Brutus' Journey	Aimee Aryal
Oklahoma	Let's Go, Sooners!	Aimee Aryal
Oklahoma State	Hello, Pistol Pete!	Aimee Aryal
Oregon	Go Ducks!	Aimee Aryal
Oregon State	Hello, Benny the Beaver!	Aimee Aryal
Penn State	Hello, Nittany Lion!	Aimee Aryal
Penn State	We Are Penn State!	Aimee Aryal
Purdue	Hello, Purdue Pete!	Joe Paterno
Rutgers	Hello, Scarlet Knight!	Aimee Aryal
South Carolina	Hello, Cocky!	Aimee Aryal
South Carolina	Cocky's Journey Through the Palmetto State	Aimee Aryal
So. California	Hello, Tommy Trojan!	
Syracuse	Hello, Otto!	Aimee Aryal
Tennessee	Hello, Smokey!	Aimee Aryal
Tennessee	Smokey's Journey Through the Volunteer State	Aimee Aryal
Texas	Hello, Hook 'Em!	
Texas	Hook 'Em's Journey Through the Lone Star State	Aimee Aryal
Texas A & M	Howdy, Reveille!	
Texas A & M	Reveille's Journey Through the Lone Star State	Aimee Aryal
Texas Tech	Hello, Masked Rider!	
UCLA	Hello, Joe Bruin!	Aimee Aryal
Virginia	Hello, CavMan!	Aimee Aryal
Virginia Tech	Hello, Hokie Bird!	Aimee Aryal
Virginia Tech	Yea, It's Hokie Game Day!	Aimee Aryal
Virginia Tech	Hokie Bird's Journey Through Virginia	Frank Beamer / Aimee Aryal
Wake Forest	Hello, Demon Deacon!	
Washington	Hello, Harry the Husky!	Aimee Aryal
Washington State	Hello, Butch!	Aimee Aryal
West Virginia	Hello, Mountaineer!	Aimee Aryal
Wisconsin	Hello, Bucky!	Aimee Aryal
Wisconsin	Bucky's Journey Through the Badger State	Aimee Aryal

Order online at **mascotbooks.com** using promo code " **free**" to receive **FREE SHIPPING**!

More great titles coming soon!

info@mascotbooks.com

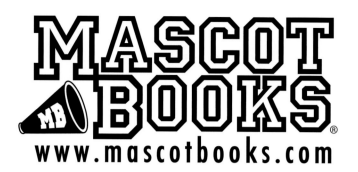
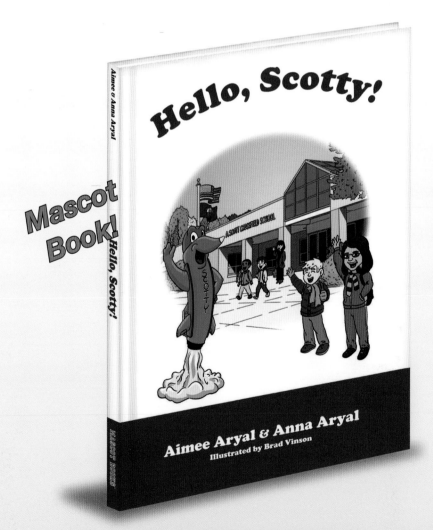

Let Mascot Books create a customized children's book for your school or team!

Here's how our fundraisers work ...

- Mascot Books creates a customized children's book with content specific to your school. When parents buy your school's book, your organization earns cash!

- When parents buy any of Mascot Books' college or professional team books, your organization earns more cash!

- We also offer options for a customized plush, apparel, and even mascot costumes!

Mascot Costumes!

Dougie the Dragon

Mascot T-Shirts!

Proud to be a Vincent Elementary Duck!

Vinny the Duck

Mascot Plush!

Lulu the Ladybug

For more information about the most innovative fundraiser on the market, contact us at info@mascotbooks.com.